Singing Diggety

by Maggie Stern

illustrations by

Blanche Sims

ORCHARD BOOKS • NEW YORK

An Imprint of Scholastic Inc.

Special thanks to Ana Cerro and Bill Reiss for
their enthusiasm, humor, and wisdom!
—M.S.

Orchard Books, an imprint of Scholastic Inc.
95 Madison Avenue, New York, NY 10016

Manufactured in the United States of America
Printed and bound by Phoenix Color Corp.
Book design by Helene Berinsky
The text of this book is set in 18 point Goudy.
The illustrations are pen and ink with watercolor.

1 3 5 7 9 10 8 6 4 2

Library of Congress Cataloging-in-Publication Data
Stern, Maggie.
Singing Diggety / by Maggie Stern ; illustrations by Blanche Sims.
p. cm.
Summary: Diggety goes to obedience school, attends a costume party, and accompanies George to school for sharing time.
ISBN 0-531-30318-7 (tr. : alk. paper)
ISBN 0-531-07179-0 (pbk. : alk. paper)
[1. Dogs—Fiction.] I. Sims, Blanche, ill. II. Title.
PZ7.S83875 Si 2001 [Fic]—dc21 00-39943

For Eddie, Mary, and Suzy with love

–M.S.

To my sister,

Mary Douglas

–love, Blanche

Contents

EXIT

Singing Diggety

George took Diggety to dog school.
A Doberman, a poodle, a bulldog, and
a pug were running around the gym.
George and the other owners sat
on stools and watched.
A basset hound in a sweater
with fluffy pom-poms came in.

Diggety ran over to the basset hound and tugged off one of the pom-poms.

"Do not do that!" shrieked the owner.

"It is hand-knit!"

Diggety chased the Doberman.

"Everyone call in your dogs," said the teacher, Natalie.

"Today we will work on 'Come' and 'Sit.'"

"Diggety, come!" George called.

Diggety grabbed the basset hound's sweater and raced across the gym.

"Drop it, Diggety!" George shouted.

Diggety did no such thing.

Natalie walked briskly to Diggety.

"Diggety, drop it," she said in a quiet but firm voice.

Diggety dropped it.

"Sit," said all the owners to their dogs.

The poodle sat down by his master's leg.

So did the bulldog.

Just when the man put down a liver treat for his bulldog, Diggety charged over and grabbed it.

"Hey, that is Herman's!" shouted the man.

“Drop it!” said George.

Diggety did no such thing.

He ate the treat in one bite, licked his lips, and then ran after the bulldog.

“Diggety, COME!” yelled George.

But Diggety was busy chasing *all* the dogs.

Natalie walked over to George.
She put her hand on his shoulder.
“At home, how do you get Diggety
to come?” she asked.
“I blow my whistle,” said George.
“He comes every time.”
George fished in his pocket and

pulled out something hard.

Only it was not George's whistle!

It was his harmonica.

He sighed.

Tears filled his eyes.

"See what happens if you blow it,"

said Natalie kindly.

George pursed his lips on the shiny metal holes.

He blew out a piercing note.

Diggety bounded over and landed at George's feet.

"AW–WHOO," sang Diggety.

George played louder.

"AW–WHOOOOO," went Diggety again.

"Diggety, stop that!" said George.

"No, wait," said Natalie.

"Keep playing."

George played as many notes as he could.

"AW–WHOOO, AW–WHOOOOOO,"

howled Diggety.

George looked around the gym.

All the dogs were sitting, ears perked,

listening to Diggety.

And so were the people.

"Diggety is singing!" George exclaimed.

"Play a tune, George," said the man
with the bulldog.
George played "Hot Cross Buns."
Diggety howled throughout
the whole song.
Natalie clapped her hands.

"You have a talented dog," she said.

She handed Diggety a liver treat.

George hugged Diggety.

"He may not *always* do what he is told,"

said George, smiling.

"But he sure can sing!"

Diggety's Costume Party

George and Lulu paced the kitchen.

George scratched his head in thought.

His sister, Lulu, scratched hers.

"Maybe Diggety could be a witch?"

said George.

"No," said Lulu.

"I think a mermaid would be better!"

"What *are* you talking about?" said their

older brother, Henry.

"You know," said George.

"The costume party for dogs!"

Henry laughed, then scratched his head.

"What about Count Dracula?" he said.

Diggety crawled under the kitchen table.

"I know!" said George.

"He can be a moose!

He can wear Lulu's

moose antler headband."

"Great idea!" said Lulu.

"And I will dress up as a dog!" said George.

Henry rolled his eyes.

"I thought the Halloween party was for

dogs," said Henry.

"So I will go as a dalmatian," said George.

At the park there was a Great Dane
with a devil's tail and red horns.

A yellow Lab wore a
pirate's eye patch.

"Look at Sumi!" cried George.
The pug dog from next door was in a pink
tutu with a ballet slipper on each paw.

"Greetings, dogs and friends!"
said the man with the whistle.
"The first event will be bobbing
for hot dogs.
Two dogs at a time.
First, the pug and the poodle.
After the games, I will give out prizes for
costumes."

The man tossed two hot dogs
into the water.
Diggety Moose loved water.
He loved hot dogs even more.
Diggety Moose pulled at the leash
and got away.
He dove headfirst into the tub of water.

“Stop that moose!” someone yelled.
“Grab his leash,” someone else shouted.
“It is not HIS turn,” called the man
with the whistle.

Diggety jumped out of the water.
He had two hot dogs in his mouth.

He shook himself.

A woman carrying her poodle screamed,

"I am all wet!"

"I am sorry," cried George.

"Diggety, DROP the hot dogs."

It was too late.

Diggety licked his lips.

“I am afraid the moose-dog must

sit out the other games,”

said the man with the whistle.

George sat down.

He held Diggety in his arms.

Diggety licked George’s face.

“George, your spots are smudged,”

said Lulu.

The man blew his whistle.
"Time to announce the winners," he said.
"The prize for most unusual costume
goes to the three-headed monster!"
The woman and her mutt took the bag of
dog food.

“The scariest costume goes to Franken-dog.”
A man and his beagle collected the giant box of dog biscuits.

“The funniest costume goes to the ballerina dog.”
Sumi, the pug dog, got a bowl with “Good Dog” written on it.

"And the prize for the cutest dog . . . ,"
said the man as
George started to walk away,
". . . goes to the dalmatian."
"There is no dalmatian here,"
someone said.

George spun around.

“I am a dalmatian,” he said.

“Do you mean me?”

“Yes, you,” said the man with the whistle.

He handed George a bone
as large as Diggety.
George beamed.
"Good job, George!"
said Lulu.
George and Diggety trotted home,
carrying the bone between them.

FA CAT

Sharing Time

George raced across the kitchen and pretended to catch a fly ball.

"Today is my sharing time at school!" he said.

"I can bring in whatever I want!"

"Are you going to bring your baseball mitt?" asked Henry.

"No way," said George.

"Your action figures?"

asked Lulu.

George shook his head.

Diggety was sniffing the floor for crumbs.

Dad picked up the juggling balls

and tossed them in the air,

one at a time.

Diggety bounded over and
caught each ball.
George smiled.
"I am going to bring Diggety,"
he said.

"Are you sure about this?" asked Mom.

George nodded.

"It is fine with Mrs. Elton.

As long as a grown-up comes in too."

Mom shook her head.

"Sorry, I am busy today," she said.

George, Lulu, and Henry turned to Dad.

"It is okay with me," Dad said.

He went to put on his tie with

all the dogs on it.

When the bell rang, Diggety charged into the classroom.

George and his dad followed.

Diggety raced over to the rabbit hutch at the back of the room.

Mrs. Elton clapped her hands.

"Time for sharing," she said.

"Today it is George's turn."

"Diggety, come," called George.

Diggety did not listen.

He sat in front of the hutch.

Sarah and Howie giggled.

"Diggety, come!"

said George again.

Diggety stared at the rabbit.

George did not know what to do!

He looked over at his dad.

Dad walked to the front of the class.

“We will begin with juggling,” he said,

“and hope for the best.”

Dad pulled out three colored balls
from his pocket.
He tossed them in the air.
He juggled them faster
and faster

until one dropped and
rolled across
the floor.
Diggety did not even sniff it.

“Diggety, please come,” called George.
Diggety pressed his nose against the hutch.

"Roll over," said George, pleadingly.

Dad glanced at Diggety.

He was nibbling the rabbit's carrot.

Dad rolled across the room.

"Chase your tail," pleaded George.

Dad spun around in circles, as fast as a top.

He stopped next to Diggety.

Diggety was licking the rabbit

through the bars.

"Shake hands!" said George.

"DO something!"

Diggety lay down.

Dad dashed around the room and shook

each student's hand.

"How original, George!" she said.

"You are the *first* to share a father!"

"Three cheers for George,"

sang the students.

Diggety woke up and ran over to George

with a juggling ball in his mouth.

He tossed it to George.

"And, George," said Mrs. Elton, smiling,

"your dog is *very* well behaved.

He is invited back *any*time."

Diggety was sleeping.

George dropped to the floor and sighed.

"That is it," he said.

"I am done."

Everyone in the class stood up

and clapped.

Mrs. Elton smiled.